RABBIT AND TORTOISE HAVE A RACE

·龟兔赛跑·

Retold by Yang Yingying
Translated by Liu Jun & Mark Ray

CHINA INTERCONTINENTAL PRESS

Little white Rabbit, with his long ears, leapt and hopped like a gust of wind. Little Tortoise, carrying his heavy shell, crawled about slowly.

Seeing Tortoise crawling
so slowly, Rabbit laughed
out loud.

"In the morning a tortoise sets
out to pick some flowers; at dusk
he still hasn't left his door."

3

Tortoise was upset by this remark. "Don't be so high-flown, Rabbit," he said. "Are you the only one who can run? I can easily outrun you!"

Rabbit couldn't help laughing. "Tortoise," he said, "you are really boastful. Why don't we have a race, then we'll see who runs faster?"

"Fine!" said Tortoise. "A race it is. I'm not afraid of you! Let's head for that tree at the foot of the hill and see who reaches the finish first."

"One, two, three, ready? Go!" Rabbit called out, then darted off with all his might. He ran so fast, a puff of dirt trailed after his tail.

7

Rabbit ran a long way and then looked over his shoulder. Tortoise had only just started.

"Tortoise dared to race against me? What a joke!" thought Rabbit, chuckling to himself.

"La la la, the victory is mine!" sang Rabbit, dancing on the road. "Why not take a nice long nap and let Tortoise get ahead? I'll pass him in no time."

Rabbit found a comfortable spot, lay on his tummy, shut his eyes and fell asleep.

Behind him, Tortoise was inching ahead.
When he finally reached Rabbit, he was almost
out of breath.

Seeing Rabbit lying there dreaming a sweet dream, Tortoise also longed for a break, but he knew that he must go on if he was going to win the race.

Carrying his heavy shell, Tortoise kept on moving.
He was exhausted, but he didn't want to stop and rest.
After a very long time, he finally reached the tree.

Rabbit woke up from his nice long nap. He stretched his arms, muttering to himself: "Tortoise must be crawling somewhere behind." But when he looked back, he thought: "Gee! Where is Tortoise?"

Rabbit swung around and looked down the road. Oh my!
There was Tortoise at the foot of the tree.

Rabbit sprang up and dashed forward, but it was too late. Tortoise had won!

Think about it, dear little readers, Rabbits do run much faster than tortoises. How did Rabbit lose the race?

xiǎo bái tù　　cháng ěr duo　　bèng ya bèng ya pǎo de kuài　　xiǎo wū
小白兔，长耳朵，蹦呀蹦呀跑得快。小乌
guī　　bēi zhe ké　　pá ya pá ya zǒu de màn
龟，背着壳，爬呀爬呀走得慢。

tù zi jiàn dào wū guī màn màn pá de yàng zi　　cháo xiào tā
兔子见到乌龟慢慢爬的样子，嘲笑它：
　　wū guī　　　wū guī　　　pá pa　　　yì zǎo chū mén cǎi huā　　wū guī
"乌龟，乌龟，爬爬，一早出门采花；乌龟，
wū guī　　　zǒu zou　　　bàng wǎn hái zài mén kǒu
乌龟，走走，傍晚还在门口。"

wū guī tīng le hěn shēng qì　　shuō　　tù zi tù zi bié shén qì
乌龟听了很生气，说："兔子兔子别神气，
nǐ yǐ wéi jiù nǐ pǎo de kuài　　wǒ kě bǐ nǐ pǎo de hái yào kuài
你以为就你跑得快？我可比你跑得还要快！"

tù zi yì tīng kě lè le shuō wū guī nǐ kě zhēn huì chuī

兔子一听可乐了，说："乌龟你可真会吹

niú pí yào bù zán men lái sài pǎo kàn shuí pǎo de kuài

牛皮！要不咱们来赛跑，看谁跑得快！"

hǎo ya sài pǎo jiù sài pǎo wǒ kě bú pà nǐ wū guī

"好呀，赛跑就赛跑，我可不怕你！"乌龟

shuō shān xia nà kē shù shì zhōng diǎn kàn shuí xiān pǎo dào

说，"山下那棵树是终点，看谁先跑到！"

yī èr sān yù bèi pǎo tù zi hǎn wán

"一、二、三，预备——跑！"兔子喊完

kǒu lìng sā kāi tuǐ jiù pǎo pǎo de zhēn kuài ya pì gu hòu bian hái

口令，撒开腿就跑，跑得真快呀，屁股后边还

yáng qǐ yí zhèn yān

扬起一阵烟。

兔子跑出好远，回头一看，乌龟才爬了一小段路呢。它心想：乌龟还敢跟我赛跑，真是笑话呀！

"啦啦啦，胜利是我的啦！"兔子高兴地跳起舞来，"不如就在这里睡一觉，让乌龟爬到前面去，我一下就能赶上啦！"

小兔子找了一个舒服的地方，把身子往地上一趴，合上眼皮，美美地睡着了。

乌龟在后边爬呀爬呀是真慢，终于爬到兔子身边时，已经累得气喘吁吁的了。

—11—

兔子睡得可真香，还在做美梦哩。乌龟虽然也想休息一会儿，可它知道只有坚持下去才会赢。

—12—

乌龟背着沉重的壳，不停地爬呀，爬呀。虽然它很累，可是一步也不敢停。爬了好久好久，终于爬到了大树下。

—13—

兔子睡了美美的一觉，伸着懒腰醒来了，心想：乌龟一定还在后面爬。可它往后一看，咦，乌龟怎么不见了？

兔子赶紧往前看，哎呀，不得了！乌龟已经爬到了大树下。

兔子着急地赶上去，可是已经太晚啦，乌龟胜利了！小朋友想一想，兔子明明比乌龟跑得快，为什么还输了比赛呢？

图书在版编目（ＣＩＰ）数据

龟兔赛跑：汉英对照 / 杨莹莹主编；刘浚译 . —北京：五洲传播出版社，2013.11（2016.3重印）
（中华传统经典故事绘本 . 童话故事篇）

ISBN 978-7-5085-2654-6

Ⅰ . ①龟… Ⅱ . ①杨… ②刘… Ⅲ . ①儿童文学—图画故事—中国—当代 Ⅳ . ① I287.8

中国版本图书馆 CIP 数据核字（2013）第 271287 号

策　　划：荆孝敏　段仁国
编　　写：杨莹莹
翻　　译：刘　浚
特约译审：Mark Ray（澳大利亚）
绘　　画：花木马工作室
责任编辑：王　莉
装帧设计：李成龙　郭　宁

龟兔赛跑

出版发行：五洲传播出版社
社　　址：北京市海淀区北三环中路 31 号凯奇大厦 B 座 7 层
邮政编码：100088
发行电话：010-82007837　010-82001477　010-82003137
制版单位：北京快乐共享文化发展有限公司
印　　刷：北京画中画印刷有限公司
开　　本：787mm×1092mm　1/12
印　　张：2
版　　次：2014 年 2 月第 1 版　2016 年 3 月第 2 次印刷
书　　号：ISBN 978-7-5085-2654-6
定　　价：19.80 元